Up, Up and Away!

DIXIE O'DAY: UP, UP AND AWAY!
A BODLEY HEAD BOOK 978 1 782 30024 3

Published in Great Britain by The Bodley Head,
an imprint of Random House Children's Publishers UK
A Penguin Random House Company

Penguin
Random House
UK

This edition published 2015

10 9 8 7 6 5 4 3 2 1

MIX
Paper from
responsible sources
FSC® C020056
FSC
www.fsc.org

RANDOM HOUSE CHILDREN'S PUBLISHERS UK
61–63 Uxbridge Road, London W5 5SA
www.randomhousechildrens.co.uk   www.randomhouse.co.uk
www.dixieoday.com

Addresses for companies within The Random House Group Limited can be found at:
www.randomhouse.co.uk/offices.htm
THE RANDOM HOUSE GROUP Limited Reg. No. 954009
A CIP catalogue record for this book is available from the British Library.
Printed in China.

Up, Up and Away!

Written by
Shirley Hughes

Illustrated by
Clara Vulliamy

THE BODLEY HEAD
LONDON

for Mark, with love from Clara

for Martha, with love from Shirley

Contents

. . . and lots more for you to find!

Today we're talking to Dixie O'Day and his friend Percy. They always manage to find adventure – wherever they are!

Hi, Dixie and Percy! First of all, can you tell us something you've always longed to do?

DIXIE: *I long to have a plane of my own. I would name it after my Aunt Daisy.*

PERCY: *I long to do ballroom dancing – on ice!*

Ah, so, Dixie, you'd love to get up, up and away! In that case, where are you both happiest: on land, on water or in the air?

DIXIE: *Well, as soon as I have got over my fear of heights, being in the air would be very exciting.*

PERCY: *Yes! As long as we remember to bring a picnic . . .*

If you could fly anywhere, where would you choose?

DIXIE: *I would fly somewhere with lots of long country walks.*

PERCY: *I would fly to a tropical island where I could relax under a palm tree with a fruity drink.*

Would you prefer to be able to fly or be invisible, and why?

PERCY: *If I were invisible I could visit my friend Dixie without Lou Ella looking crossly out of her window at me.*

DIXIE: *I would love my car to be able to fly – what an adventure that would be!*

And finally tell us a time you were especially brave.

DIXIE: *I prefer to be modest about it, but I did rescue our friend Mr Canteloe when he fell into the sea.*

PERCY: *And I stuck up for Dixie in the school play when he forgot his words, so I ran on stage and joined in loudly!*

Well done, Dixie and Percy — you are brave adventurers — and thank you!

Ariel
likes:
playing the trumpet
playing chess
ice-skating

Lou Ella
likes:
fast cars
new things
getting her own way

Lou Ella's
Friends
like:
afternoon tea

Bill the
Balloon Man
likes:
balloons

The Police
like:
keeping the roads
crime-free

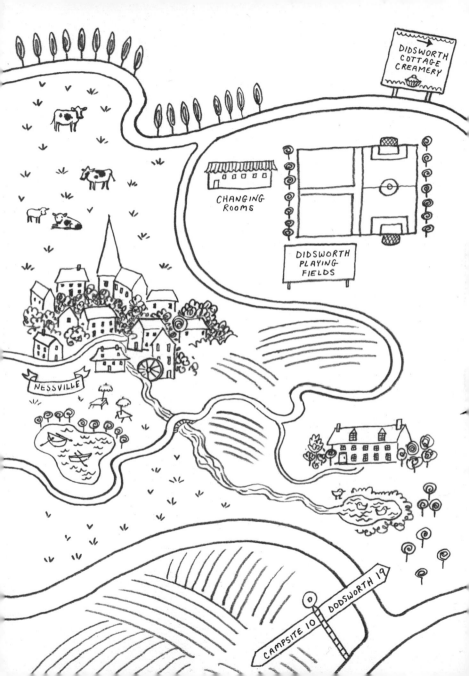

Chapter One

DIXIE O'DAY

Dixie O'Day was very proud of his car. He cleaned and polished it every weekend and his friend Percy came to help.

DiXiE O'DAY

One Saturday, when they were
giving it an extra shine, Dixie said:

'This is a really good car, but one
day I'd like to try a different form of
transport.'

'It still goes well,' said Percy
encouragingly. But he added, 'As long
as you don't try to overtake in the fast
lane.'

Dixie's car had given trouble
recently when, during a slow crawl
home from the shops, the engine had
failed during a traffic jam, and he and
Percy had ended up pushing it all the
way home.

DIXIE O'DAY

Don Barrakan at the garage had repaired it in no time, of course.

But even so there were times when Dixie daydreamed about being effortlessly airborne – up, up and away!

Up, Up and Away!

Dixie's irritating next-door neighbour, Lou Ella, bought an expensive new car every year. She liked new things: new clothes, new cars, new furniture and new kitchen cabinets. She even changed her pets quite often.

DIXIE O'DAY

She had already tired of the
goldfish because she thought he was
boring,

and the Siamese cat because he
sharpened his claws on the fitted carpet,

and the hamster because he kept her awake at night running and running on his little wheel.

She had given them all away, to her friends, one by one.

Now she had bought
a parrot, which she was
teaching to speak. His name
was Ariel.

She had spent a lot of
money on a beautiful parrot
perch, which she placed
in the bay window of her
house so that passers-by
could see her interesting
new pet.

And she devoted a lot of time to grooming him, glossing up his feathers and manicuring his claws. Ariel endured this in pained silence.

She even took him for rides in her car, though Ariel simply sat hunched in the seat beside her.

She was always trying to get him to talk, but Ariel refused to say a word.

Her friends called round to admire him.

'Can he talk?' they asked.

'Oh yes,' Lou Ella answered, 'of course he can. But he's a bit shy in company.'

DiXiE O'DAY

Privately she went on urging him to speak,

but she was not
a patient lady.

14

'Come on, why don't you say
something? The man at the pet shop
assured me that you were a very good
talker. So why don't you say "Pretty
Polly" or "Who's a clever boy, then?"
as other parrots do?'

But Ariel remained stubbornly
silent, sitting on his perch.

DIXIE O'DAY

One morning, when Percy was helping Dixie to shore up a bit of collapsing trellis near Lou Ella's garden wall, they saw Ariel pacing restlessly up and down.

Up, Up and Away!

'Good morning!' Dixie called out.
And, to his surprise, Ariel answered:
'Good morning to you, sir!'

'I didn't know you could speak!' said
Dixie in astonishment.

DIXIE O'DAY

'Of course I can,' Ariel replied. 'But
I just don't care for Lou Ella's boring
conversation. She keeps trying to
make me say silly, pointless things.
She doesn't seem to realize that I am
a highly educated bird. It's too humili-
ating! My confidence is getting so low
I've almost forgotten how to fly.'

After this they often chatted together over the garden wall when Lou Ella was out. And they soon discovered that Ariel was indeed a very interesting bird . . .

DIXIE O'DAY

. . . with many hidden talents.

Chapter Two

DIXIE O'DAY

On Saturday morning Percy came hurrying round to Dixie's house bursting with excitement and waving a leaflet.

'Look at this, Dixie! It's an announcement about a big Air Show, right here in Didsworth!

DIDSWORTH
AIR SHOW
displays·flights·teas

today!

Up, Up and Away!

It's on at the playing fields today.
There are all sorts of aircraft –
gliders, helicopters, hot-air balloons!
Come on, we mustn't miss it!'

DiXiE O'DAY

As they were leaving, Dixie caught sight of Ariel hanging about in the garden as usual.

'Why don't you come with us?' he cried. 'Quick! Before Lou Ella sees us!'

Up, Up and Away!

Ariel needed no encouragement.
He hopped joyfully
over the gate

and they all
set off together.

DIXIE O'DAY

They arrived at the Air Show,
where they found a wonderful sight.
There were so many different kinds
of aircraft on show.

People were queuing up for demonstration flights. Big crowds gasped and cheered as they took off.

DiXiE O'DAY

One of the biggest attractions was the hot-air balloons, now tethered to their baskets and floating gently like great coloured Easter eggs.

Dixie had always dreamed of learning to fly and imagined jumping into the cockpit of his own aircraft and taking off . . .

. . . until he remembered how scared he was of heights.

The three friends wandered around, fascinated by all the exhibits. Ariel turned out to be very know-ledgeable about all types of aircraft. Early flight was one of his specialities.

DiXiE O'DAY

Meanwhile Lou Ella, back at her
house, had discovered that Ariel
was missing. She had searched every
room and all over the garden but
he was nowhere to be found.

'That wilful bird!' she muttered.
'He must have gone off somewhere
without asking my permission.'

She went out and looked up and
down the road. Then she caught sight
of the leaflet that Percy had dropped,
lying near Dixie's front gate. She
picked it up and read it.

DIDSWORTH
AIR SHOW
displays·flights·teas

today

DIXIE O'DAY

'So that's it!' she exclaimed. 'I bet Dixie and Percy have gone off to see the Air Show and have taken Ariel with them! It's just the sort of thing they'd do. Well, I'll soon fetch him back!'

Up, Up and Away!

And she put on her special motoring hat, jumped into her car and zoomed off.

By this time Dixie, Percy and Ariel
had managed to edge right up close
to one of the hot-air balloons.

Up, Up and Away!

The friends watched the sandbags being removed and one of the men in charge adjusting the guy ropes.

They were so fascinated that they were quite unaware of Lou Ella in her car, edging determinedly through the crowd, tooting her horn angrily.

DIXIE O'DAY

She was getting closer and closer,
and she was almost upon them
when Ariel spotted her.

Up, Up and Away!

'Quick! It's Lou Ella!
Don't let her catch me!'
he squawked, and
dived into the
balloon basket.

Dixie and Percy
vaulted in too and
crouched down.

But Lou Ella had already caught sight of them! She jumped out of her car and elbowed her way through the crowd towards the balloon.

Chapter Three

Just as Lou Ella reached them, there came a sudden gust of wind. The guy ropes of the great balloon had been left undone, and it began to take off – slowly at first, then rapidly gaining height – up, up and away!

DiXiE O'DAY

'Now we've done it!' said Percy grimly. But Ariel was delighted. He was strutting up and down along the edge of the balloon basket, flapping his wings in triumph.

'We're off! We're off! You can't catch us now!' he squawked.

They looked down at the faces of
the crowd, fast receding below. There
was Lou Ella, purple with rage,
shouting something that they were
already too far away to hear.

It was a beautiful day. The sky
was full of little fluffy clouds. A brisk
wind soon carried the balloon high
above the town, over the rooftops and
out into the countryside beyond.

They had no idea where they were
heading or how to steer, but for a
while they were happy to just drift
along.

DIXIE O'DAY

Dixie discovered that if they pulled a certain rope, the balloon went upwards, and if they pulled another, it went down. They could not make it go faster or slower. So for the moment they decided that the best way to go was UP.

Ariel gallivanted about, sometimes perching on the edge of the basket, opening his wings wide, and sometimes hanging upside down from one of the guy ropes.

Meanwhile Dixie and Percy
leaned over the side, watching
the shadow of the balloon
tracking them below.

After a while Percy said:

'It must be nearly lunch time. It's a pity we didn't bring a picnic!'

'What we need is an island to land on,' exclaimed Ariel. 'Like the one I lived on long, long ago, when I could fly, with lots of fruit and nuts and a sparkling stream of fresh water.'

DIXIE O'DAY

'Good idea!' said Dixie. And he
added: 'If we can find one, that is . . .'

Chapter Four

But now the weather was changing.
The sun disappeared behind dark
clouds and it began to rain. It was
hard to see where they were going or
what was below.

Up, Up and Away!

Soon Dixie and Percy were soaked through and shivering, but Ariel did not seem to mind being wet. He spread his wings wide, fluttered upwards and strutted up and down . . .

'Here we go, into the bright blue yonder!
Flying high, happy and free!'

'Bother the blue yonder,' muttered Dixie, peering anxiously into the grey mist that was gathering below. 'I think we should try to land.'

His fears seemed justified when there was a sudden loud crack of thunder overhead and a flash of lightning ripped through the sky.

Up, Up and Away!

Now the rain came down in torrents, beating against the balloon and soaking them all.

The high wind was making the
balloon rock dangerously. Percy
clung to the side of the basket, while
Ariel hung onto the rigging with his
claws.

Up, Up and Away!

Dixie was desperately trying to bring the balloon down, but he couldn't see anywhere to land. At last he saw some bright lights and – yes! – something that looked like an island!

DiXiE O'DAY

They began to descend and, more by luck than good navigation, landed right in the middle of it.

Chapter Five

Cautiously, they climbed out of the basket and looked about them. They were surrounded by dripping bushes and a few trees, but from quite nearby they could hear the steady rumbling of heavy traffic.

'I don't think this looks quite like the kind of island I was hoping for,' said Ariel. 'It looks more like a traffic island to me!'

He was right. Instead of being surrounded by clear blue water, all they could see was an endless stream of trucks, cars and motorcycles roaring past. None of them stopped. They were all too intent on reaching the motorway.

'Looks as if we're all
stuck here for a bit,'
said Dixie.
'Oh dear!'
squeaked Percy.
'And it's been
such a long
time since
breakfast!'

Their first
thought was
to secure
the balloon to a tree, then shelter
as best they could under the bushes.

The storm was now showing signs
of easing up. The lightning had
stopped, but the rain still came down
relentlessly.

They were all soaked to the skin.
Dixie felt in his pockets, hoping
he might find a bar of chocolate he
had forgotten about. But there was
nothing.

DIXIE O'DAY

'Perhaps we could rig up some kind of shelter to keep the rain off for a bit,' he suggested as cheerfully as he could.

They all set to work. Ariel collected twigs and leaves, and the other two brought fallen branches and tried to make them stand up like a wigwam.

Up, Up and Away!

But they were not very good at
it, and despite all their efforts it
collapsed in a heap.

'I wish I'd paid more attention
when we learned this kind of
thing in the Didsworth Forest Folk
Fellowship,' said Percy.

'Though I did get commended for
my egg custard,' he added.

'I'm afraid that's not much help to
us now,' said Dixie rather shortly.

DiXiE O'DAY

They huddled together, waiting for the rain to let up, and listening to the roar of the traffic.

At last they heard the sound of a car slowing down and the tooting of a horn. They rushed through to the edge of the bushes.

Up, Up and Away!

There was a car parked
there all right . . .

73

DiXiE O'DAY

. . . it was Lou Ella's car! She had leaped out and was standing right beside it, arms akimbo!

Chapter Six

DiXiE O'DAY

'Come here AT ONCE, Ariel!'
shouted Lou Ella. 'I've wasted
enough time following you and your
friends all over the place in that silly
hot-air balloon. Now you're coming
home with me, my boy!'

But now, to her
astonishment, and
for the first time
in their relationship,
Ariel spoke to her.

'No, I will not! In my
view you are a highly
unsuitable person to own
a pet, and I have no wish
to belong to you, no
matter how luxurious
your home is. And
to tell the truth, your
conversation bores
me stiff!'

Lou Ella was flabbergasted!
Then she lunged at Ariel. He let
out a wild squawk and flew
high up into a tree.

But for Dixie and Percy there was
no such means of escape. Lou Ella
had them cornered.

At that moment they heard the piercing wail of an approaching police car. It drew up sharply, right behind Lou Ella.

DiXiE O'DAY

Two traffic officers got out and strolled towards her. She had quite forgotten that she had parked her car on a traffic roundabout.

Quickly, she put on a false smile and tried to apologize.

'I was just going to move it!' she cried, but it was no use. One of them was already bringing out her notebook.

Dixie and Percy seized their chance. They raced back to the hot-air balloon and Dixie leaped inside to prepare for lift-off. Ariel flew down and perched on the edge of the basket. But just as Percy was about to scramble aboard, there came a great gust of wind and the balloon started to take off.

DIXIE O'DAY

'Wait for me!' shouted Percy. But it was too late. The balloon was already rising fast into the air. Dixie leaned out of the basket as far as he dared and held out his hand to Percy. Their fingers touched, but then they were pulled apart.

'Don't leave me!' cried Percy, terrified.

Ariel reacted swiftly. He picked up
a rope that was lying in the bottom of
the basket and flew down with it in
his beak. Percy caught hold of it as
Dixie grasped the other end.

DIXIE O'DAY

The basket rocked dangerously as, just in time, Dixie managed to pull Percy inside. He landed in a breathless heap.

Ariel flew up after him, very pleased with himself, squawking:

'Did you see me *fly!* Talk about quick off the mark!'

Up, Up and Away!

As they rose higher and higher,
leaving the traffic island behind,
they looked down on Lou Ella, who
was being given a parking fine
and a severe ticking off
by the police.

DIXIE O'DAY

Her motoring hat had fallen awry,
but she was still protesting shrilly:
   'It was only for a minute or two,
I tell you!'

Chapter Seven

DIXIE O'DAY

It was late afternoon by now. The rain had cleared at last.

'Time we were getting home,' said Dixie. 'If the wind will blow us in the right direction, that is.'

Luckily it did. But as they drew near to the familiar landmarks, Ariel's mood changed and he became very quiet, sitting on the side of the basket.

Dixie and Percy noticed that a
great many birds had now begun
to gather and were flying alongside
them, keeping pace with the balloon.
Among them were some small
parakeets.

They were especially animated,
swooping around and over them in
splendid formation, like a squadron
of aeroplanes.

DIXIE O'DAY

Ariel began an earnest
conversation with them.

At last he turned to Dixie and
Percy and said:

'My friends, I'm afraid the time
has come for me to leave you. I can't
possibly go back to live with Lou Ella.'

'You would be very welcome to come and live in my house,' Dixie offered.

But Ariel shook his head politely. 'Thank you, no. I'm afraid it wouldn't do. She would always be close by with her silly chatter; it would be very bad for my nerves. Thanks to your comradeship on this adventure— I have regained my confidence to spread my wings and fly again.'

DIXIE O'DAY

'Where will you go?'

'Well, I have been talking to my good friends here, the parakeets. They have made a home on a delightful island not far from here – NOT a traffic island, I can assure you – one with plenty of fruit and nuts and a stream of clear water, and they have invited me to join them. They are

keen to improve their language skills
and I think I can help them there. So
I have decided to go with them.'

'We will miss you!' said Dixie.

'I'll keep in touch.
The parakeets are very
helpful in delivering
notes and letters.'

DIXIE O'DAY

It was sad to say goodbye. Dixie and Percy watched as Ariel launched himself into the air and joined the great flock of birds, wheeling and calling and making a great clamour in their joy at flying free.

Dixie sighed as he watched them disappearing towards a bank of gold-edged clouds.

'It must be jolly nearly supper time!' said Percy.

Luckily the wind continued to
blow them in the right direction.
When at last they arrived back at the
playing fields, Bill the balloon man
helped them to land without difficulty.

'You've been out a long time,' he
said. 'I was beginning to get worried
about you.'

Dixie and Percy strolled home-
wards together.

'What a big adventure!' said Dixie.
'It's sad that we won't be seeing Ariel
next door any more, but he will be far
happier on his island. We might even
visit him there one day.'

DIXIE O'DAY

'I feel we've been away for a lot longer than just a day, don't you, Dixie?' said Percy. 'And I'm SO hungry! Let's stop at the Didsworth Cottage Creamery for tea and cakes before planning what to cook for supper!'

Up, Up and Away!

When at last they returned to
Dixie's house, they saw Lou Ella
lurking in her front garden. She gave
them a furious look over the hedge.

DIXIE O'DAY

'Where's Ariel?' she demanded.

'Ariel? Oh, he won't be coming
back. He's found a much better
place to live and so he's decided
to leave you.'

'Good riddance!' replied Lou Ella.
'As a matter of fact I've spoken to
the man in the pet shop already. I've
decided to get a nice obedient rabbit
next.'

DIXIE O'DAY

'If Lou Ella does get a rabbit, I don't envy him,' muttered Dixie as they opened the front door.

'Perhaps we can help him burrow his way out!'

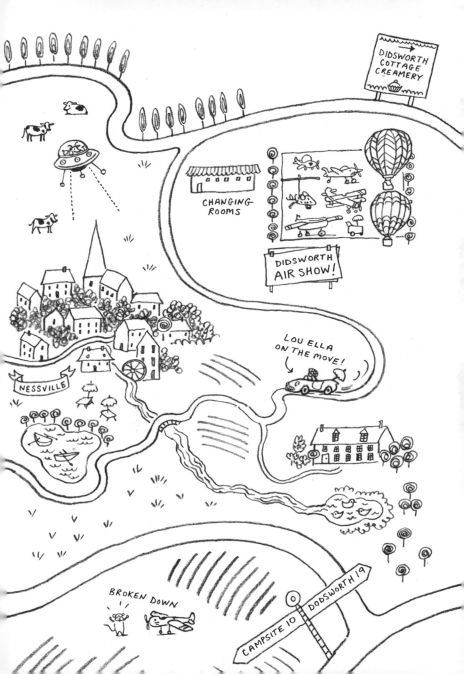

Shirley is Clara's mum, and together they have created Dixie and Percy's adventures. Let's find out more about them!

Hello, Shirley and Clara!

Like Dixie and Percy, can you tell us something you've always longed to do?

Shirley: I've always longed to be able to sing (in tune!)

Clara: I wish I could go in a hot air balloon, just like Dixie and Percy.

Now, would you prefer to be able to fly or to be invisible, and why?

Clara: I would prefer to be invisible, so I could get up close to the fiercest animals like tigers and bears.

Shirley: I would prefer to fly, as I do in my dreams.

If you could fly anywhere, where would you choose?

Shirley: Somewhere warm and sunny, as long as I could be home by bedtime!

Clara: Me too. We could travel by hot-air balloon - hold onto your hat, Mum!

Tell us about your pets; do they have any special talents like Ariel?

Shirley: I have no pets now, but I used to have a tabby cat called Leggy.

Clara: I have a goat called Lucky. He doesn't live in my house, but with lots of other goats in the country. His special talent is that he can spell: if I spell out loud B-R-E-A-K-F-A-S-T, he comes running over!

And finally, tell us a time when you were especially brave.

Clara: In P.E. lessons when I was young, because I couldn't do any of the sports.

Shirley: When, at school, I told the playground bully to get lost.

Wonderful, Shirley and Clara— thank you for sharing your brave moment with us!

Dixie and Percy's Games

Dixie and Percy get stuck on a traffic island in the rain – they don't even have a bar of chocolate with them! Here are some games for you to play if you're stuck without a pen and paper or a ball.

THE NAME GAME

Pick a category, like animals or countries. One person goes first and names a country (if that's what you've picked). The next person has to name a country that begins with the last letter of the country named, and so on. Dixie and Percy play this with pop stars – and Percy always chooses Peaches Miaow!

WHICH HAND?

Choose a small item that fits into the palm of your hand. Put both hands behind your back, then hold the item in one of your closed hands. When you bring your fists to the front, your opponent must guess which hand the item is in.

WHISPERS

One person whispers a short story – two or three sentences – to the next person, who then has to whisper the same story to the next person. Once the story has been whispered around all the people, the last person says what they have heard. You'll be amazed how different it is from what was originally whispered!

I WENT SHOPPING . . .

One person starts by saying, 'I went shopping and I bought a cream cake.' The next person says, 'I went shopping and I bought a cream cake and a gingerbread man.' Each person adds a new item, and must remember the items that went before. What kind of silly items can you dream up? When Dixie and Percy play, Percy always gets very hungry, because he always chooses delicious things to eat!

SCISSORS, PAPER, STONE

Two people make a fist with one of their hands, then they count to three. On three, both make one of three shapes: Scissors (two fingers sticking out, cutting like scissors), Paper (fingers flat and touching each other, like a sheet of paper), or Stone (fingers curled in a fist). In every combination there is a winner and a loser:

Scissors beat Paper (because they cut it).
Paper beats Stone (because it wraps around it).
Stone beats Scissors (because it blunts them).

Fabulous Flying Machines

Now it's your turn! Can you draw your own fabulous flying machine?

How many wings does it have? And what colour are they? Does it fly like a bird, or soar like a balloon?

How many people will fit inside your flying machine, and how high will it go?

The sky's the limit!

When you've come up with your design, go to **www.dixieoday.com** to find out how to send your drawing to Dixie!

The Dixie O'Day Quiz

Dixie has written a special quiz
to test you! How much can you remember
about *Dixie O'Day: Up, Up and Away!*

I. Who repaired Dixie's car?

2. Where is the big Air Show held?

3. True or false: Percy is scared of heights.

4. True or false: Dixie, Percy and Lou Ella float away
in the hot-air balloon.

5. Where did Ariel used to live?

6. True or false: they land on a traffic island.

7. Do they have any food with them on their
adventure?

8. Who was in the Didsworth Forest Folk Fellowship?

9. True or false: Bill the balloon man catches
up with the balloon first.

10. Who gets a parking ticket?

11. Who goes to live with the parakeets?

12. Where do Dixie and Percy go for tea and cakes?

If you enjoyed

DIXIE O'DAY
Up, Up and Away!

then you'll love Dixie and Percy's

next adventure

DIXIE O'DAY
and the
Haunted House

Turn over for your first chapter . . .

DIXIE O'DAY

and the Haunted House

Dixie was planning a camping holiday and he invited his friend Percy to join him.

'What we need is the simple life, Percy!' he said. 'We won't go to a campsite with all those cafés and table tennis and showers with hot running water. We'll go somewhere where there are no other people and we can be alone with nature!'

'Sounds great,' Percy agreed. But he added: 'Nothing wrong with a nice hot shower, though!'

On the morning of their departure, Dixie got up very early. After a quick breakfast, he began packing the boot of his car with a small tent, two sleeping bags and ground sheets, a portable cooking stove and a few basic provisions.

It was some time before Percy arrived. He was loaded down with all sorts of things, including books, a radio, a Scrabble set, his ukulele and plenty of chocolate.

'Surely we don't need all that?' said Dixie. 'This is supposed to be the simple life, remember?'

But Percy firmly packed them onboard.

Dixie's nosy neighbour, Lou Ella, had come to her front gate to watch.

'I hope the weather stays fine for you,' she said. 'The forecast on the radio said it was going to rain later.'

Dixie and Percy ignored her. She was still standing there watching them as they drove off.

They drove for several hours with Dixie at the wheel. Percy read the road map.

At last they left the motorway behind and reached some beautiful open countryside. They saw a sign pointing to the Happy Down Camp-site, but Dixie sped past. As they did so Percy caught a glimpse of the friendly family, Mum, Dad and the three little ones, settling down in their comfortable camper van, with hot showers near at hand, and a shop in case they needed extra supplies, and he felt a small pang of envy. But Dixie kept going, and soon they turned into a winding lane with high hedges on either side.

They passed only one house, a

very old one, set well back from the lane behind unkempt bushes. Its walls were covered in ivy, and its uncurtained windows looked out blankly from beneath a tumble-down roof.

'I don't much like the look of that place,' said Percy. 'Doesn't seem like there's anyone living there. A bit spooky, if you ask me.'

They turned into a winding lane with high hedges on either side, and kept going until at last Dixie stopped the car by a five-barred gate. They both got out and peered over it into the field beyond.

'This looks just right,' said Dixie enthusiastically. 'I do believe there's a stream down there by those trees. It's an ideal spot!'

Right away he scrambled through a hole in the hedge.

'You begin unpacking the car, Percy,' he called back. 'And I'll pile our things up on this side. Then we'll pick out a really good place to pitch our tent.'

Neither of them had noticed the sign near the gate which read:

STRICTLY PRIVATE – KEEP OUT!

TRESPASSERS WILL BE

PROSECUTED!

But Dixie and Percy's camping trip
won't all go to plan. There are terrible
calamities and spooky happenings awaiting
our daring duo – and things that go
bump in the night . . .

Will Dixie and Percy find out the truth
about the old dark house?

Find out in

DIXIE O'DAY
and the Haunted House